GIORGIO
The Train That Wanted To Ride a Boat

Pictures and story by Anita Benarde

Weekly Reader Books
MIDDLETOWN CONNECTICUT

To Andrea, Dana, and Scott, with love

Publishing, Executive, and Editorial Offices:
Weekly Reader Books
Middletown, CT 06457

Giorgio is a train. Every day he gets up bright and early, warms up his engine, and chugs into Campiglia Maritima Station to pick up passengers. Then he heads for Piombino-by-the-Sea.

1

2

Campiglia and Piombino are little towns
on the west coast of Italy. Giorgio had been
going back and forth between them for as long
as he could remember. Whenever he passed Signor
Filippi's vineyard, he gave a long whistle and a short
toot. Then he puffed up the big hill past the ancient
town of Populonia, gave a sigh when he reached
the top, and fairly flew down into the valley
that led to Piombino.

Giorgio put on his brakes very carefully. He didn't want to upset the baskets of food that almost all his passengers carried. When he stopped at the pier, everyone rushed to get off. Some people wanted to be the first to get their tickets. Others wanted to have drinks and ice cream as they waited for the boat that would take them to Elba . . . and their holiday.

Giorgio watched from the station as the boat docked. The crowd cheered, "Bravo! Bravo! Bravo!" as the boat drew near.

4

Then the people went on board, and the boat sailed away. For a little while after the boat left, Giorgio could still hear its passengers laughing and singing. Then all was quiet. Giorgio turned around and headed back to Campiglia. *If only I could ride a boat!* he thought. The idea made him so excited, he almost jumped off the tracks. "RIDE A BOAT, RIDE A BOAT," his wheels seemed to say.

"RIDE   RIDE   RIDE
    A   A   A
     BOAT. . .   BOAT. . .   BOAT,"

they clacked away. As Giorgio passed Signor Filippi's vineyard, he almost forgot to whistle.

Back at the roundhouse, Giorgio couldn't stop repeating

"RIDE   RIDE   RIDE
     A   A   A
       BOAT. . .   BOAT. . .   BOAT. . . ."

Giorgio didn't know he was talking out loud until the Sette-bello Express laughed and said, "You ride a boat? Trains ride on tracks, not on boats. Giorgio, you are a silly little train."

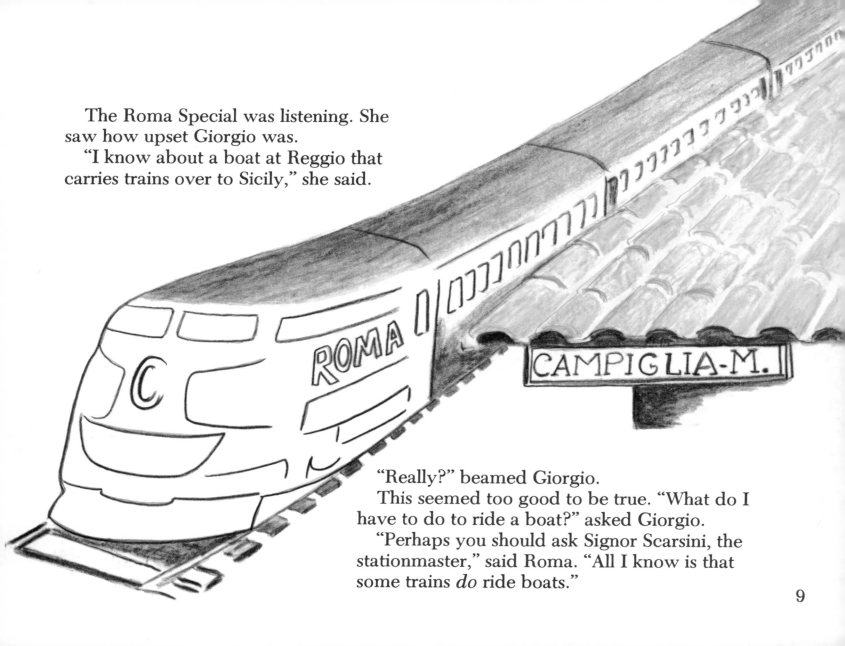

The Roma Special was listening. She saw how upset Giorgio was.

"I know about a boat at Reggio that carries trains over to Sicily," she said.

"Really?" beamed Giorgio.

This seemed too good to be true. "What do I have to do to ride a boat?" asked Giorgio.

"Perhaps you should ask Signor Scarsini, the stationmaster," said Roma. "All I know is that some trains *do* ride boats."

9

"Ride a boat? The one at Reggio? H-m-m," mused the stationmaster. "As far as I'm concerned, you can go. You've done a good job."

10

Giorgio almost exploded with happiness.

"But I can't just send you off to Sicily without a good reason," the stationmaster added. "I'll let you know as soon as I find a reason."

"Oooh," sighed Giorgio, disappointed.

11

Now the trip to Piombino seemed to take forever. And to make matters worse, Giorgio's wheels seemed to make only one sound . . . "ride-a-boat, ride-a-boat, ride-a-boat." Giorgio was miserable.

ride-a-boat..... ride-a-boat..... ride-a-boat.....

   As the weeks crept slowly by, the stationmaster said
nothing. Giorgio began to believe that he would never get to
ride a boat.

13

Summer turned to fall. Fall was the most beautiful time of the year. The grape harvest was one of the best. Everyone else seemed so happy, it was hard for Giorgio to be sad.

14

One Saturday as Giorgio pulled into Campiglia, Signor Scarsini was standing on the station platform, waving his hands furiously and shouting, "Giorgio, Giorgio, I have great news! The Populonia School needs a train just your size to take the children all the way to Siracusa in Sicily. Do you still want that boat ride?"

16

"Still want my boat ride? Yes, oh yes!" Giorgio answered, so excited he could hardly get out the words.

On Tuesday evening, dozens of boys and girls from the school climbed aboard Giorgio. The little train was sparkling. The workers had done an extra special job of cleaning him that day. As Giorgio pulled out of the station, everyone shouted, "BUON VIAGGIO, GIORGIO! BUON VIAGGIO!— Have a wonderful trip!"

Down the beautiful coast of Italy went Giorgio and all his passengers. They passed the big city of Roma as well as tiny seaside villages. It was fun seeing all the sights. But Giorgio couldn't wait to get to Reggio. It was only an hour away and that's where he'd get to take the boat ride.

Then it happened. . . .

A warning light flashed on the tracks. "Slow down" was its message. *But why?* thought Giorgio as he carefully rounded the easy curve into the town of Cirello.

Ahead of Giorgio the whole town seemed to be gathered on the tracks. As Giorgio came to a complete stop at the red light, he could see the trouble.

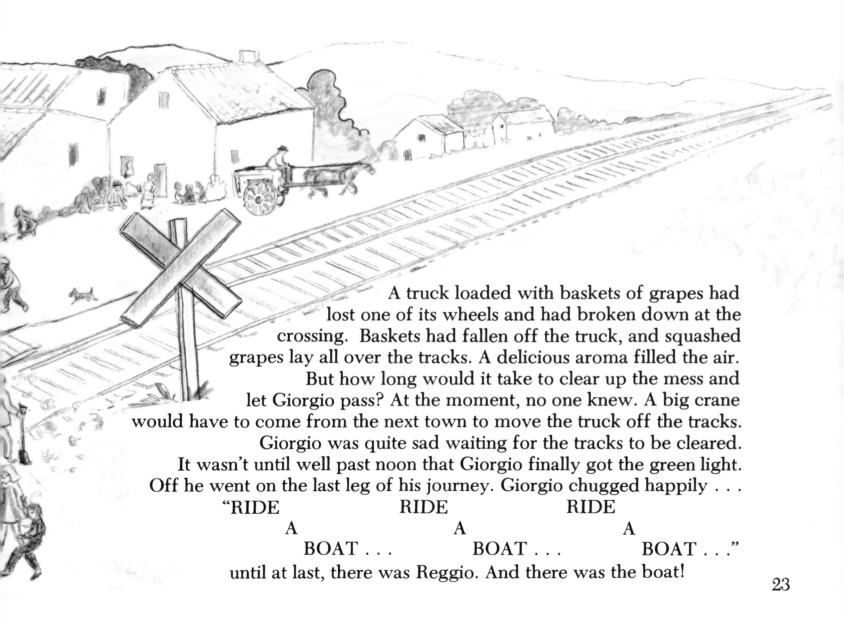

A truck loaded with baskets of grapes had lost one of its wheels and had broken down at the crossing. Baskets had fallen off the truck, and squashed grapes lay all over the tracks. A delicious aroma filled the air. But how long would it take to clear up the mess and let Giorgio pass? At the moment, no one knew. A big crane would have to come from the next town to move the truck off the tracks. Giorgio was quite sad waiting for the tracks to be cleared. It wasn't until well past noon that Giorgio finally got the green light. Off he went on the last leg of his journey. Giorgio chugged happily . . .

"RIDE   RIDE   RIDE

A   A   A

BOAT . . .   BOAT . . .   BOAT . . ."

until at last, there was Reggio. And there was the boat!

Giorgio watched excitedly as all the children and other passengers boarded the boat. Then he watched the cars drive on. *Will there be room left for me?* Giorgio wondered. But at last, Giorgio chugged on board too.

Giorgio could hear the big engines stir to life beneath him. Then there came two sharp blasts from the ship's whistle as the ship moved out of the harbor. Giorgio liked the sounds he heard, the engines, the whistle—and the slap-slap-thud of the waves against the boat. How curious and pleasant it was! Giorgio wiggled his caboose with joy!

"Is this your first trip?" asked the train riding next to him.

"Yes," said Giorgio, very pleased with himself.

"If you look out of that porthole," the first train added, "you'll be able to see all the different boats. There's a lot to see on this ride."

Giorgio didn't miss a thing. And how he hated to leave the boat when it arrived in Sicily. He was having too good a time. But he could hear the children calling. "Avanti, avanti, Giorgio!—Let's go."

Giorgio laughed. "You want to get to Siracusa as much as I wanted to ride a boat! But how lucky I am. I'll have another ride on the way back home!" With these happy thoughts, off they all went, singing. The children sang "To Siracusa we will go," while Giorgio's wheels hummed a new tune . . .

"I RODE A BOAT . . . RODE A BOAT . . . RODE A BOAT."